SP BR CAMARENA
Camarena, Cathy, 1966-
Frida y Franco /

**PALM BEACH COUNTY
LIBRARY SYSTEM**
3650 Summit Boulevard
West Palm Beach, FL 33406-4198

Frida y Franco

Cathy Camarena, M.Ed., and Gloria B. Ruff, M.Ed.

Consulting Editors
Lourdes Flores-Hanson, M.S.E., and Gloria Rosso-White

Published by ABDO Publishing Company, 4940 Viking Drive, Edina, Minnesota 55435.

Copyright © 2006 by Abdo Consulting Group, Inc. International copyrights reserved in all countries. No part of this book may be reproduced in any form without written permission from the publisher. SandCastle™ is a trademark and logo of ABDO Publishing Company.

Printed in the United States.

Credits
Curriculum Coordinator: Nancy Tuminelly
Cover and Interior Design and Production: Mighty Media
Child Photography: Steven Wewerka, Wewerka Photography
Photo Credits: AbleStock, Comstock, Photodisc

Library of Congress Cataloging-in-Publication Data

Camarena, Cathy, 1966-
    Frida y Franco / Cathy Camarena, Gloria B. Ruff.
       p. cm. -- (Primeros sonidos)
    ISBN 1-59679-863-7 (hardcover)
    ISBN 1-59679-864-5 (paperback)
    1. Spanish language--Vowels--Juvenile literature. I. Ruff, Gloria B., 1971-
II. Title. III. Series.
  PC4155.C365 2006
  468.1'3--dc22

                                                                                                                       2005025388

SandCastle™ books are created by a professional team of educators, reading specialists, and content developers around five essential components that include phonemic awareness, phonics, vocabulary, text comprehension, and fluency. All books are written, reviewed, and leveled for guided and early intervention reading, and designed for use in shared, guided, and independent reading and writing activities to support a balanced approach to literacy instruction.

Let Us Know

After reading the book, SandCastle would like you to tell us your stories about reading. What is your favorite page? Was there something hard that you needed help with? Share the ups and downs of learning to read. We want to hear from you! To get posted on the ABDO Publishing Company Web site, send us e-mail at:

sandcastle@abdopub.com

SandCastle Level: Beginning

fr

ABCChDEFGH
IJKLLLMNÑOP
QRSTUVWXYZ

abcchdefgh
ijklllmnñop
qrstuvwxyz

Frida

Franco

fruta

fresa

frijoles

Mira el .

Mira la ____ .

La 🍓 es roja.

Mira los .

Esta es una 1/4.

Franco tiene frijoles.

A Franco le gusta comer frijoles.

Frida tiene fresas.

Las fresas son rojas.

Los frijoles y las fresas están en el frasco.

¿Cuáles de estas cosas comienzan con **fr**?

Más palabras que comienzan con fr

franjas

fregadero

frenos

frío

fruncir

About SandCastle™

A professional team of educators, reading specialists, and content developers created the SandCastle™ series to support young readers as they develop reading skills and strategies and increase their general knowledge. The SandCastle™ series has four levels that correspond to early literacy development in young children. The levels are provided to help teachers and parents select the appropriate books for young readers.

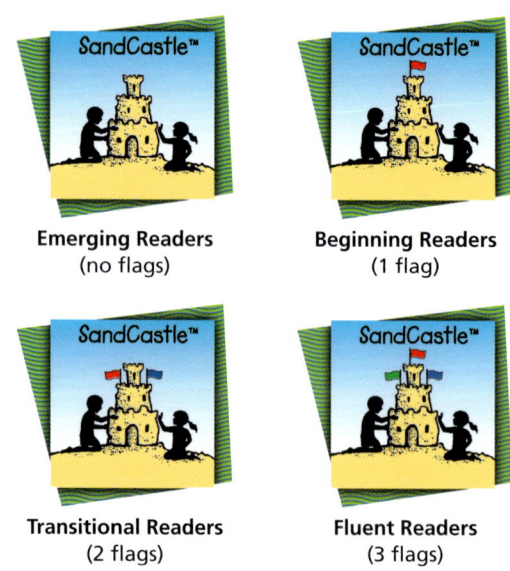

Emerging Readers
(no flags)

Beginning Readers
(1 flag)

Transitional Readers
(2 flags)

Fluent Readers
(3 flags)

These levels are meant only as a guide. All levels are subject to change.

To see a complete list of SandCastle™ books and other nonfiction titles from ABDO Publishing Company, visit **www.abdopub.com** or contact us at:
4940 Viking Drive, Edina, Minnesota 55435 • 1-800-800-1312 • fax: 1-952-831-1632